To the people who made this story possible: my beloved children, Dena, Jonah, Benjamin, and Rikki, who all looked after the sheep; my much-adored Aunt Frannie and Uncle David, who welcomed the lamb Moses to their Passover seder; The PJ Library; my agent, Kendra Marcus; and my wonderful editor, Naomi Kleinberg
—L.E.M.

To my family
—T.M.-W.

Text copyright © 2013 by Linda Elovitz Marshall. Jacket art and interior illustrations copyright © 2013 by Tatjana Mai-Wyss. All rights reserved. Published in the United States by Random House Children's Books, a division of Random House, Inc., New York.

Random House and the colophon are registered trademarks of Random House, Inc.

Visit us on the Web! randomhouse.com/kids

Educators and librarians, for a variety of teaching tools, visit us at RHTeachersLibrarians.com

Library of Congress Cataloging-in-Publication Data
Marshall, Linda Elovitz.
The Passover lamb / by Linda Elovitz Marshall ; illustrated by Tatjana Mai-Wyss. — 1st ed.
p. cm.
Summary: Miriam has especially looked forward to the Passover seder at her grandparents' home because it is her first year to ask the four questions, but the unexpected arrival of triplet lambs complicates her family's plans.
ISBN 978-0-307-93177-1 (trade) — ISBN 978-0-375-97106-8 (lib. bdg.) — ISBN 978-0-375-98107-4 (ebook)
[1. Passover—Fiction. 2. Seder—Fiction. 3. Sheep—Fiction. 4. Animals, Infancy—Fiction. 5. Jews—Fiction. 6. Farm life—Fiction.] I. Mai-Wyss, Tatjana, ill. II. Title.
PZ7.M35672453Pas 2013 [E]—dc23 2011052092

MANUFACTURED IN CHINA
10 9 8 7 6 5 4 3 2 1
First Edition

The Passover Lamb

By Linda Elovitz Marshall
Illustrated by Tatjana Mai-Wyss

Random House ⌂ New York

One morning, as Miriam scattered chicken feed and gathered eggs, she chanted, "*Ma nishtana ha-laila ha-zeh...?* Why is this night different from all other nights?"

After weeks of practice, she knew the words and melody by heart. Tonight at her grandparents' house, she would sing the Four Questions at the seder, the special Passover meal. She could hardly wait.

Next, Miriam fed the sheep.

They all came running when she called.

Except for one . . .

Snowball!

Miriam peered into the barn. Snowball was
still inside, pawing the floor, moving hay and
straw with her nose.

Something's not right, Miriam thought.

She ran toward the house.

"There's something wrong with Snowball!"
she called.

Her parents and her brother, Aaron, hurried to the barn with Miriam. Snowball was grunting and breathing hard.

Miriam looked again at the big sheep. "Maybe she's having a baby," she said.

"I think you're right," said her father, "though it *is* late in the season. But Snowball's so woolly, we didn't notice."

"Well, I hope she has the baby soon," Aaron grumbled.

"Oh, no!" Miriam cried. "I almost forgot. We're leaving. . . ."

"We've still got things to do before we can go," their mother said.

"Let's finish getting ready."

After lunch, Miriam returned to the barn.

As she tiptoed in, she heard the soft sounds a mother sheep makes to her newborns. In the dim light, she saw Snowball nuzzling two tiny lambs.

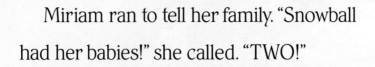
Miriam ran to tell her family. "Snowball
had her babies!" she called. "TWO!"

The family rushed to the barn. As they watched Snowball
nursing the twins, Aaron pointed to a dark lump in the hay.

"What's that?" he asked.

Far from Snowball and the newborns, a third baby lamb
was lying all alone.

Miriam carried him to his mother.

Baaaa-AAAA! Snowball grunted. She pushed him away with her nose and turned back to the other two lambs.

"Snowball, this one needs you, too," Miriam whispered.

Again, Snowball shoved the little lamb aside.

"She might not have enough milk for all three babies," Miriam's mother said. "He might have to be fed with a bottle."

Miriam knew that orphaned lambs needed milk every four hours. No one else would have time to care for him, not even the neighbor who looked after the animals when Miriam's family was away. That meant they might have to stay home. They would miss the seder.

"Please, Snowball," Miriam begged. "Take care of your baby. *Pleeeeeease.*"

"Let's leave them for a bit," Miriam's mother suggested. "Maybe Snowball will change her mind."

Later, the family returned to the barn.

The little lamb was still alone, calling for his mother.

"He's starving!" Miriam cried. She grabbed a bottle and filled
it with special milk for newborn lambs. Holding him gently,
Miriam fed the hungry lamb.

"Miriam, honey," her father began, "I'm very sorry, but there's no way we can leave him." He sighed. "Mom and I will get things ready for a seder at home."

"No!" Aaron shouted. "I want to see Grandma and Grandpa."

Miriam frowned. "And it's my year to ask the Four Questions," she said. "I've been practicing for weeks. I want the whole family to hear."

Alone in the barn, Miriam cuddled the lamb.
She felt like crying.

The lamb looked up at her. *Maaaa-aaaa,*
he bleated. *Maaaa-aaaa!*

"I don't know what to do," Miriam told him. "I can't leave
you, but I want to be at Grandma and Grandpa's for Passover.
We'll tell the story of how the Jews were slaves in Egypt and
a wicked king named Pharaoh made them work night and
day. One mother hid her baby, Moses, in a basket to save him.
When Moses grew up, he led the Jews to freedom."

Miriam stood up.

"Hey!" she said, giving the lamb a hug. "I know what to do!"

A short while later, Miriam was ready. "Let's go!" she called.

In her arms was a basket. And nestled in the basket, wearing a diaper with his tiny tail sticking out, was the little lamb.

Miriam's father laughed. "Great idea!" he said. "And we've got just enough time to get there for the start of the seder."

"Yippee!" Aaron cheered.

At last, Miriam and her family arrived at her grandparents' house.
"Look, everyone!" Miriam said as she proudly carried the basket
into the house. "Meet Moses."

As the whole family celebrated the Feast of Freedom,
Miriam chanted the Four Questions perfectly. And Moses,
the Passover lamb, reclined in her lap.

Maaaa! he bleated softly. *Maaaa!*

Miriam giggled. "Listen!" she said. "He's singing

the Four Questions, too! *Maaaa! nishtana …*"

Author's Note

The Passover Lamb was inspired by an actual event that took place on my farm. One year, just before the beginning of Passover, a sheep refused to nurse one of her newborn lambs. As in the story, my children fed him from a bottle. When it was time to leave for the seder, they diapered him and brought him along. As a gentle joke, they named him Moses.

During the seder, Moses was passed from one lap to another (or placed under the table, where he nibbled our feet) as we told of the Jewish people's escape from slavery in Egypt. As is customary, the storytelling began when the youngest capable child—that year, one of my daughters— sang the Four Questions in Hebrew.

The Four Questions begin with *one* question: Why is this night different from all other nights? That question branches into four others: Why, on *this* night, is matzo eaten? Why, on *this* night, are bitter herbs eaten? Why, on *this* night, is food dipped twice into something else? And why, on *this* night, do Jews recline at the Passover table?